The Bremen Town Musicians

A Retelling of the Story by the Brothers Grimm

Retold by
Leah Osei

Illustrated by
Tracie Grimwood

Lee Aucoin, *Creative Director*
Jamey Acosta, *Senior Editor*
Heidi Fiedler, *Editor*
Produced and designed by
Denise Ryan & Associates
Illustration © Tracie Grimwood
Rachelle Cracchiolo, *Publisher*

Teacher Created Materials

5301 Oceanus Drive
Huntington Beach, CA 92649-1030
http://www.tcmpub.com
Paperback: ISBN: 978-1-4333-5601-8
Library Binding: ISBN: 978-1-4807-1723-7
© 2014 Teacher Created Materials
Printed in China
YiCai.032019.CA201901471

Contents

Chapter One

The Road to Bremen

Once upon a time, a farmer had a donkey that had served him for many years. Donkey carried sacks of grain to the mill and potatoes to the market.

3

As the years passed, Donkey grew old and weak. He could no longer serve the farmer well. The farmer decided he must send Donkey far away. Donkey was very sad that this was to be his reward for having been such a faithful worker.

Donkey was worried until an idea came to him. "I know," he cried, "I will go away. I will run to Bremen and become a musician."

Chapter Two

Escape!

Donkey ran across the field, jumped over the fence, and ran along the road to Bremen, singing happily as he went.

After a while, he saw something by the side of the road. It was a very old, sad-looking dog. Donkey asked, "Why are you sad, Dog?"

Dog replied, "Every day, I grow older and weaker. I can no longer round up sheep for my master. He is planning to send me away."

"Well! Why don't you run away with me to Bremen and become a musician?" asked Donkey.

"Yes! I'd like that," said Dog, wagging his tail.

Donkey and Dog set off along the road, singing happily as they went.

Chapter Three

Along the Road

Soon, they saw something in the distance.   Together, they moved closer.

It was a very old, sad-looking cat sitting by the side of the road.

Donkey asked, "Why are you sad, Cat?"

Cat replied, "Every day, I grow older and weaker. I can no longer catch mice. My mistress is planning to send me away."

"Well! Why don't you run away with us to Bremen and become a musician?" asked Donkey.

"Oh, yes!" said Cat, jumping onto the road and stretching her body.

Donkey, Dog, and Cat set off along the road, singing happily as they went.

Chapter Four

Past the Farm

Soon, they saw something in the distance. It was a very old, sad-looking rooster perched on top of a farm gate.

Donkey asked, "Why are you sad, Rooster?"

Rooster replied, "Every day, I grow older and weaker. I can no longer wake my mistress each morning. She is planning to send me away."

"Well! Why don't you run away with us to Bremen and become a musician?" asked Donkey.

"Yes, please," said Rooster, flapping his wings in excitement.

Donkey, Dog, Cat, and Rooster set off along the road, singing happily as they went.

Chapter Five

Friends

On and on they traveled, until they were so tired they could go no farther. "Let's spend the night here," said Donkey as he leaned against a tree.

Dog and Cat lay down. Just before he fell asleep, Rooster saw a light glowing in the distance. "I can see a cottage! It looks quite close!" he called.

"Let's go and see. Maybe we can sleep there," said Donkey.

When they reached the cottage, Donkey crept to a window and looked in. "There's a table with lots of food on it. But it looks like the house has been robbed. There are some mean-looking men inside. Looks like they took over the house," he whispered.

"Sounds dangerous," Rooster said.

"Or wonderful. I wish we were in the house where it's warm," said Dog.

"How can we get rid of the robbers?" asked Cat.

Donkey thought. Then, an idea came to him. He placed his front feet on the window ledge and called, "Dog, sit on my back! Cat, sit on Dog's back! Rooster, perch on Cat's back! When I give the signal, everyone sing."

When they were in position, Donkey gave the signal, and they began singing. Donkey brayed. Dog barked. Cat meowed. Rooster crowed.

Chapter Six

Terrible Sounds!

The friends made such a noise that the glass in the window shattered onto the floor. Rooster went flying into the cottage. Cat jumped in after him, and Dog and Donkey tumbled in, too.

Animals and men were everywhere. The robbers thought a huge monster had burst in on them. They ran away as fast as they could. The friends got to enjoy a warm meal. Soon, they settled down to sleep. It *was* wonderful.

But when all was quiet, the men returned. One robber slipped in through the window. Watching Cat, the robber thought he saw glowing coals and held a match to them. He expected the match would light. But the coals were really Cat's glowing eyes! Cat flew in his face, spitting, hissing, and scratching.

The noise woke up Dog. He bit the robber's leg. Then, Donkey kicked the robber so hard he flew up to where Rooster was perched.

Rooster crowed loudly, "*Cock-a-doodle-do!*"

"I'm getting out of here!" the robber cried. "There's a horrible witch in the house who spat at me and scratched my face. And by the door, there's a man who stabbed me in the leg. And on the floor, there's a monster that beat me. And in the roof sits a judge with a voice as terrible as the wind!" Well, at least that's what the robber thought.

The robbers were so afraid that they ran away, never to return. The four friends stayed in the cottage. From there they made a short journey every day to Bremen, where they became famous musicians.